W9/16

APR   2011

11/17

Last Ride

Laura Langston

orca soundings

ORCA BOOK PUBLISHERS

Library and Archives Canada Cataloguing in Publication

Langston, Laura
Last ride / Laura Langston.
(Orca soundings)

Issued also in electronic format.
ISBN 978-1-55469-417-4 (bound).--ISBN 978-1-55469-416-7 (pbk.)

I. Title. II. Series: Orca soundings
PS8573.A5832L38 2011   JC813'.54   C2010-908053-X

First published in the United States, 2011
Library of Congress Control Number: 2010942085

Summary: Tom struggles to give up street racing
after killing his best friend in a race.

*Orca Book Publishers is dedicated to preserving the environment and has printed
this book on paper certified by the Forest Stewardship Council.*

Orca Book Publishers gratefully acknowledges the support for its publishing
programs provided by the following agencies: the Government of Canada
through the Canada Book Fund and the Canada Council for the Arts,
and the Province of British Columbia through the BC Arts Council
and the Book Publishing Tax Credit.

Cover design by Teresa Bubela
Cover photography by Getty Images

ORCA BOOK PUBLISHERS
PO Box 5626, Stn. B
Victoria, BC Canada
V8R 6S4

ORCA BOOK PUBLISHERS
PO Box 468
Custer, WA USA
98240-0468

www.orcabook.com
Printed and bound in Canada.

14 13 12 11 • 4 3 2 1

For Barry

Every end is a new beginning.

—Proverb

Chapter One

I killed my best friend. Thirteen months and six days ago.

Not on purpose. It was an accident. Even the cops wrote it up that way. But if I hadn't dared Logan to race, he'd still be alive.

Sometimes I swear I see him. Out of the corner of my eye. Just a glimpse.

Like he's haunting me. Like he's royally pissed.

That accident…I think about it every day. And most nights too.

I'm in Ray's garage, flat-backing it under a 350Z and silently cursing because the hoist is taken, when I feel it. Breath on the side of my face.

I bolt up too fast and hit my head on the undercarriage.

"Whoa, man, I didn't mean to spook you." Ray's beady squirrel eyes peer in at me. He's a paunchy middle-aged guy in greased-up coveralls. He has thinning hair and dirty mechanic's hands. "Get your ass out from under there. I need you to do a test drive."

My heart's still racing as I wriggle out from under the 350Z, grab a rag from the floor and wipe my hands. Sweat trickles between my shoulder blades. I'm warm but I still shiver. I'm not sure if it's the cold air blasting through the open garage door or the idea of the test drive. Maybe it's a little of both.

Ray nods his head at the car waiting outside the service bay. "I've installed a new turbo in that baby. She's gonna fly."

That means somebody somewhere is missing the turbo charger for his Lexus…or maybe his entire car is gone.

Ray drops the keys into my palm. "Go on. Take it around the block."

I stare at the black IS300 Lexus. Logan died in his dad's brown one.

"Make sure you push it into the double digits." Ray smirks. "You know you want to."

Of course I want to. I haven't broken thirty since the accident. I think about racing all the time. The adrenaline rush, the power, the blur of speed. Followed by the screech of tires and the explosion of metal.

This must be how an addict feels. Craving something they know is deadly.

I toss my rag in the bin and head for the door. "I'll be back in fifteen minutes."

"Take at least half an hour. And don't be a wimp. Remember what I said the other day: use it or lose it."

Ray's trying to suck me back in. He wants me to race again. Ray's a slime-ball. And coming from me, that's saying something. Because, in spite of what my mom believes, I'm a badass.

The leather seat crackles when I slide behind the wheel. Was it this cold when Logan slid behind the wheel of his dad's Lexus thirteen months ago? I can't remember.

But it's cold in Kent now. In fact, the whole Pacific Northwest is having record lows for November. We even had snow the other day. I turn the key and the engine burbles to life. I flick on the heat, adjust the mirrors, switch on the wipers. When I pull out of the lot, the headlights sweep over my silver Acura. The one Ray and I just finished rebuilding. The one I'll be paying for forever.

Ray's garage is in a large ten-block industrial park on the edge of Kent. The surrounding buildings are dark, and the streets are deserted. No surprise for eight thirty on a Thursday night. It's the ideal time to put a car through its paces. I'm nervous at first, which is unusual for me behind the wheel. Driving is where I'm most at home. It's the steel shell I need between me and the world.

After about five minutes of driving up and down the blocks, I relax. I let the engine creep to sixty, then seventy, then eighty. Buildings rush by. I'm one with the car, loving the feel of the wheel under my hands, the slick sound of the tires slapping the wet pavement.

Suddenly I feel it. The tiny prickle at the back of my neck that makes me think Logan is watching. My heart leaps.

I take my foot off the gas, hit the brakes. I can't do this again. Can't. Do. This. Speed killed Logan. I killed Logan.

And I won't ever let myself forget it.

I've only been gone fifteen minutes, and Ray will give me a hard time if I return too soon, so I head a few miles east, away from the industrial park, toward Mulligan's Ravine. I pass a run-down strip mall, a performance garage that's Ray's biggest competition, and a Dairy Queen. When my cell phone vibrates, I pull over to read the text.

It's Aisha. *Where R U?* I read. *We're at Drew's. U coming?*

Maybe in a while, I text back. But I'm not going to the party. Hannah will be there. Probably with Cole. And seeing Hannah is too damned hard. I slap the phone shut, shove it in my pocket and head for Ray's.

That's another reason I'm a badass. I have the hots for my dead buddy's girl. How disgusting is that?

The light ahead flashes amber, then red. I gear down, coast to a stop at the intersection and adjust my wipers. The rain has turned to a mean, sleety drizzle. It suits my mood. Hannah's been spending too much time with Cole. And I've been spending too much time thinking about her.

I turn on the radio, punch the buttons, search for some mind-numbing rock. A car pulls up beside me. I'm too busy channel surfing to care.

Until I hear the rev of an engine.

Until I hear the signal.

I glance to the left, see two guys in a silver Nissan.

The driver smirks and revs the engine a second time.

Sweat blooms on my palms.

If he knew about Logan, would he still want to race?

Probably.

Hell, *I* still want to race.

But I won't.

I pull my gaze away, punch button number three on the radio and crank the volume.

The guy revs his engine again. This time his passenger yells something.

My head snaps up just in time to hear the second insult. "Wuss."

My spine stiffens. I might be an ass but I'm no wuss.

I don't look at them. Forcing my shoulders into a slouch, I pretend not to care. But my foot is poised, my eye is on the light.

The second I sense the green, I floor it, launching away from the intersection a good car length ahead of them. There's no time for doubt, just the exhilarating blur of the world flying by, the amazing sense of control as I weave the IS300 effortlessly around an suv like it's a piece of trash in the middle of the road. Blood roars in my ears, makes me light-headed, giddy with power.

The past, the future—they fall away. Nothing matters but this. I'm in the zone. At one with my steel shell. Focused on the here and now. More focused than I've been in a long time.

I'm back where I belong.

And then I catch a flash of movement out of the corner of my eye. It's a guy and a dog, heading for a side street. I do a double take. It's Logan. Staring right at me.

And the smell of cherry Twizzlers floods the car.

My foot falls off the gas. The two jerks in the Nissan shoot past, waving their hands out their open window. I'm shaking too much to care.

Logan is haunting me. Either that or I'm crazy.

Chapter Two

I'm not crazy. I'm imagining things.
I turn down the side street to follow the
guy and the dog. The guy looked just
like Logan.

But there's nobody there. All I see is a
lone dog sniffing the base of a tree. The
same dog I saw a minute ago.

The same dog Logan was standing
beside.

My shaking kicks into high gear. The smell of the Twizzlers Logan loved threatens to choke me. Slowly I cruise down the block past the dog. Sleet hits the windshield with tiny *pings*, making it hard to see. I turn the wipers up to high and peer into the darkness. I'm searching for a body. Signs of life.

Nothing.

After about three blocks, my shaking stops and the smell of the Twizzlers fades. I turn the car in the direction of the garage.

Mom says I'm overly sensitive. I've picked up on other people's feelings since I was a kid. Only it's gotten worse since the accident. She calls it being an empath. That's just a fancy word for feeling too much.

But the only thing I'm feeling right now is scared. I saw Logan. At least I *think* I saw Logan. Maybe it was a trick of light? Or maybe I'm just tired? I haven't been sleeping a lot lately.

Punching down my fear, I focus on the other thing that's bugging me. How could I let myself be conned into racing again?

Because racing is what you do, my badass self says. *It's who you are.*

Not true, I repeat over and over again until I almost believe it. *That's not true.*

"You finally got some color in your cheeks," Ray says with a broad grin when I pull in a few minutes later. "That's all it takes to bring you back to life. A little pedal to the metal. How much did you push 'er?"

"Don't know." I toss the keys in his direction. "I wasn't exactly looking at the speedometer."

A broad grin cracks his face. "Now that's what I like to hear."

A white blur peels around the corner and squeals to a stop within inches of Ray's back door. I jump back. When I realize what I'm looking at, my heart goes into overdrive. It's a shiny new Porsche Boxster. Top-of-the-line sexy. A whole lot of show but not much go. Not the kind of car I ever see at Ray's.

The driver door opens. A short muscular guy in jeans and white T-shirt jumps out. I stare at his upper arm. If I had a thunderbolt tat that big, maybe I'd wear T-shirts in the middle of winter too.

Ray takes another drag from his cigarette before grinding the butt under the toe of his work boot. "Your pay's in the envelope," he says to me. He angles his head toward the desk in the corner. "I'll see you tomorrow."

I head for the desk.

"Santiago!" Ray turns to the Porsche owner. "I thought you weren't getting here until next week." Santiago answers, but I'm too busy counting my cash to catch what he says.

"What the hell?" I must have made a mistake. I count again.

No mistake. It's a measly hundred and thirty-one bucks. I was banking on four hundred. Hoping for five. I need gas money, spending money, and I wanted to give Mom a few hundred bucks toward my medical bills. "Uh, Ray, there's a mistake here."

Ray and I have a sweet deal going. Since I'm not a licensed mechanic, Ray pays me under the table, sometimes in cash but sometimes in parts for my car. "I don't need any more parts, remember? The Acura's fixed."

"How could I forget? You owe me up the wazoo for it."

My heart knocks against my ribs. It's the third time this week he's brought up my debt.

He waves his hand dismissively through the air. "That's all I'm giving ya."

Like hell. I close the distance between us. "I worked twenty-seven hours this week. That's worth two hundred and seventy bucks. And I sent three guys in. One wanted a complete rebuild on the front end. That has to be worth five hundred."

That's the other deal Ray and I have. I refer people to his shop, and he kicks back a percentage of whatever they spend. And they spend big. Mostly because Ray will do whatever they want to improve the performance of their cars, whether it's legal or illegal. Safe or unsafe.

"What three guys? I didn't see nobody."

Santiago is watching us, a tiny smile on his thin lips. He's older, at least thirty. He looks tough but he's not. When his gaze connects with mine, a shiver crawls down my spine. The guy's naïve. And somehow Ray's conning him.

I hate knowing stuff about people. But I also hate being cheated. "Blair said he was coming in for a new front end."

"He didn't show up. Nobody did." Ray grabs my arm and steers me back toward the desk. "Listen, Shields, you're lucky I paid you anything at all. You owe me twenty thousand dollars in parts alone for the rebuild on the Acura. And then there's the bodywork I shopped out and paid for."

I don't like where this conversation is going. "I know."

"I'm not gonna carry you anymore."

Sweat blooms on the palms of my hands. "What are you saying?"

"You aren't working enough hours to pay off your debt, what with going to school and all." A muscle in his jaw twitches. "Either you come up with five grand by the end of next week or I take your car."

My stomach bottoms out. "But it's my car. The title's in my name." Off in the distance, someone laughs. Logan. I turn hot, then cold. "You can't take it away."

Ray's beady squirrel eyes bore into me. "Sure, I can. I've got twenty grand worth of bills proving what you owe me. It won't be hard convincing a judge to sign it over."

He can't be serious. "You wouldn't go to court. You hate lawyers and judges." And anything else to do with the law.

"Try me."

Words jam the back of my throat. I'd rather cut off my right arm than give up my Acura, and he knows it. "I can't come up with five thousand dollars in a week. You know that." Even if I could, there's no way I'd give it all to Ray. It wouldn't be fair to Mom. She's been working major overtime to pay down my medical bills. I'd have to give some of it to her.

"Either you bring me five grand in cash or you bring in ten grand worth of business."

"Ten grand in a week?" Mentally I start adding up the costs of various jobs. "It's almost December. Guys aren't spending on cars. They're saving up for gifts and stuff."

"That's your problem, not mine."

"Come on, man! Be reasonable."

"Oh, I am." He smiles. "'Course, there is another way you can make money."

Racing, he means. "I told you, I'm not racing again." I promised Hannah I wouldn't. Right after she visited me in the hospital.

"Then you've got two choices. You either deliver five grand in cash or ten grand worth of business. By the end of next week. Or that car is mine."

Ray is not getting my Acura. No way. I need to find him ten thousand dollars' worth of business. Starting tonight.

And that means I'm going to a party.

Chapter Three

There's a great road on the way to Drew's place. Guys hang around all night just waiting for an opportunity to race. I go fifteen minutes out of my way to avoid it.

You can't stop, my badass side taunts when I turn onto Drew's street. *Not now. Not when your car's on the line.*

Yes, I can, my mind argues. *I'll find ten grand in business. Starting with Blair.*

I *can't* lose my Acura. I pull in behind a gray Taurus and kill the engine. My gaze drifts over my black leather seats, my new stereo system with navigation and DVD screens, my custom gauges. You'd think I'd want to get rid of my car after what happened. Not true.

I stare out across the carbon fiber hood. Losing it won't bring Logan back. Although half the time it's like he's back anyway. I swear I feel his eyes on me as I get out of the car and follow the sound of the music.

Drew's curtains are open. People are dancing in the living room. I'm halfway up the stairs before I spot Hannah. She's dancing with Cole, laughing up at him. My heart hammers against my rib cage. Cole Murray. The poster boy for perfect.

Aisha flings open the front door and grabs my arm. "Tom! 'Bout time you got here."

Cole glances my way. When our eyes connect, he smirks. Cole considers me a waste of air space. Underneath Cole's superiority, I pick up another feeling: his yearning for Hannah. He likes her as much as I do.

But only one of us can have her. Only one of us deserves her.

I drop my gaze and let Aisha pull me into the house. The overpowering smell of smoke and booze hits my nose. Good thing Drew's parents aren't back from Mexico until Saturday. It'll take days to clear the air.

"Wanna dance?" Aisha slurs. She's all over me, like hot wax on a car. Hannah hasn't noticed. She's still focused on Cole.

"In a minute." I survey the crush of bodies, looking for Blair. I need to talk to him about his front end. Convince him Ray's the guy to do the job.

"Oh, come on!" Aisha tugs on my arm, and my stomach flips. Her perfume smells like rancid cookies.

I ease out of her grip. "Have you seen Blair?"

She pouts and gestures beyond the archway to the dining room. I spot a bunch of guys grouped around an oval table, doing shooters. "He's back there with Drew and the rest of them."

"I'll catch you later." Careful not to go anywhere near Hannah and Cole, I weave through the dancing bodies toward the dining room.

"Shields!" Drew bellows when he catches sight of me. He's holding a bottle of tequila in one hand, a shot glass in the other. He's surrounded by half a dozen guys, including Blair and Lucas. Lucas was supposed to bring his Civic into the shop for transmission work. Good. I can hit them both up at once.

"Where were you? I expected you hours ago."

Of course he did. I used to be the first to arrive and the last to leave. "I was at the shop working on an engine." I direct my words to Blair, but he and Lucas are laughing hysterically about an episode of *South Park* and aren't paying attention.

Drew shoves a glass at me. "Here." He gestures to the lime wedges and saucer of salt on the table. They're surrounded by beer, vodka, mix and chips. "Get set up," he adds. "We're celebrating."

"Yeah? Thanksgiving was last week. What's the occasion?"

I'm stalling. Don't get me wrong, I like tequila. A lot. It's a great way to kill pain. I glance over my shoulder, glimpse the back of Cole's head. It helps me shut out what everybody else is feeling too. I need that. Sometimes a lot. But drinking tequila makes me stupid. My gaze settles on Hannah. And she hates it.

"I've done my admissions applications," Drew says when I turn around. "Three suckers all filled out." He belches. The stench of beer and tequila makes me reel backward.

"Only three?" Geoff skips the salt and goes straight for the tequila. "My old man made me do five. Plus apply for a pile of scholarships." He downs his shot.

I don't want to talk about college admissions and SATS and scholarships. It reminds me of Mom and the mess we're in. The mess I created.

"Here, man." Drew rubs lime on a shot glass, dips it in salt, tops it with tequila. "Drink up." He presses the glass into my hand.

"I'd rather have a beer." I can nurse a beer all night, drive home without worrying.

Blair snaps to attention. "I'll take your tequila then." He plucks the glass from my hand.

I grab a Bud and pop the tab but don't drink it. "I thought you were coming in to get your front end done?"

"Change of plans." Blair flips a chunk of his too-long red hair out of his eyes. "There's this guy my brother knows. With a tricked-out Lancer. He has an awesome mechanic up in Everett who does all sorts of neat crap—"

"Like Ray," I interrupt.

"Exactly." He grins, completely misses my point. "I'm thinking about getting him to do my front end."

"You'd drive forty miles to get your front end done?" Of course he would. I drove almost two hundred miles once just for a special set of rims.

Blair nods.

"I might take my trannie to him too," Lucas adds.

My breath catches. No way. A trannie job's worth a few thousand to me. He has to bring it to Ray. "Don't be crazy.

Ray's *it* when it comes to trannie work. He'll do whatever you want. You know that."

"Yeah, but apparently the mechanic in Everett is something else." Lucas shakes his head. "That Lancer can really go."

"My Acura really goes too. Ray's done a crapload of work on it."

"How would we know?" Lucas laughs. "You haven't raced it in a year."

Blair pours another shot. "That's because Shields thinks he's jinxed."

I suck back some beer. Not jinxed. Just not stupid anymore.

"Quit being a wuss," Lucas says. "Come out and show us what you can do."

Wuss. I hate that word.

Drew scowls. "Leave him alone."

Drew's the only guy I know without a car. He borrows his dad's pickup sometimes, but mostly he's without wheels.

That's why he holds so many parties. If he didn't, he'd be a total loser.

"There's a race tomorrow night," Blair says. "The Lancer'll be there. I'll text you the details."

I'm about to remind him that I'm not racing anymore when I feel that tiny prickle at the back of my neck again. Like someone is watching me. I glance over my shoulder and see short blond hair and Logan's St. Christopher medallion.

Hannah. She's thinking of Logan.

I can tell by the twist of pain on her face. For once, I'm not. I'm thinking only of her. How it felt when she touched my sore leg in the hospital. How it made me feel things I have no right to feel.

"Whatdaya say, Shields?" Blair presses.

I open my mouth to answer, but Aisha interrupts. "There you are!" She plants a wet, sloppy kiss on my cheek.

"Come on. I love this song." She plucks the beer from my hand, slams it on the table beside a bag of ripple chips and presses against me. "Let's dance."

A flush fills my cheeks. Hannah's eyes widen. Cole's eyes are trained on Aisha's breasts, which are practically spilling out of her tank top.

"Shields?" Blair yells. "You haven't answered. Tomorrow night? You coming or not?"

Hannah's gaze burns. She wants me to say no. She expects me to say no. But I need to go to the race. I need that Lancer to lose. I need the guys to bring their cars to Ray. "I'm coming," I say as Aisha leads me away. "But I won't be racing."

Laughter and a few good-natured insults follow us. They aren't as painful as the look of disappointment in Hannah's eyes. She doesn't believe me. She thinks I'm lying.

She's wrong.

Chapter Four

Mom corners me a few hours later when I sneak in the front door.

"You're late."

I peer across the hall into the living room. She and her boyfriend, Cam, are on the couch, framed by the glow from the yellow and orange Tiffany lamp.

"Sorry." I flip the dead bolt on the door and walk across the hall. "There was a party at Drew's. Didn't you get my message?"

"Yes, but it's a school night." The circles under Mom's eyes look purple in the pale light. "And you have a curfew."

"I drove some friends home. It took longer than I thought." Mostly because I had to pull over twice so Aisha could throw up.

Cam gives me a silent salute. I nod back. Cam never says much, but he never criticizes either. That's worth a lot.

"I worry, Tom. You know that."

"Yeah." Guilt stings. "I'm sorry," I repeat.

"Mr. Lansky called. He's concerned about your performance in senior seminar."

Oh man, I don't need Lansky on my case. Not when I'm worrying about my car.

"Senior seminar is important," Mom adds. "It prepares you for life after high school."

Like three months of classes can prepare you for the rest of your life. I manage, just barely, not to roll my eyes. I glimpse a smirk at the corners of Cam's lips too.

"He says you missed the appointment he set up to discuss your college applications. And you didn't write your SAT test either."

"I told you last month, I'm not going to college." At least not the kind of college Mom has in mind. Technical college is way cheaper. I can become a mechanic and be earning money in two years. And that reminds me...I dig in my pocket, pull out five twenties and put them on the coffee table. "For the bill."

My medical bill. That'll maybe take it down to eighty thousand nine hundred. Big whoop. But at least it's something.

Mom's eyes soften. "You don't have to do that."

A lump the size of a small engine clogs my throat. Maybe not, but Mom can't pay the whole thing herself. "I know."

"But you do need to write your SAT," she says gently. "And talk to Mr. Lansky about scholarship applications."

"A scholarship won't cover it all. You know that from Becky." My sister took out a student loan and is working two jobs to cover her second year.

"We'll figure something out, Tom. Don't worry about it. In the meantime, get some sleep. You look tired."

How can I sleep with Ray's threat hanging over me? With Lansky's phone call?

My feet are heavy as I drag them up the stairs. I reach the landing and start up the last few steps, and that's when I hear it. A chuckle in my ear.

I whirl around. Logan!

But there's only empty space in front of me. And the faint, unmistakable scent of the cherry Twizzlers he loved to chew.

My fingers are shaking so much it takes me three tries to start up the computer. *Need for Speed 2* is a poor substitute for the kind of racing I want to do, but it will stop me from imagining things. It'll keep me busy. And awake. Which means Logan won't be able to invade my dreams.

"Nice of you to join us, Mr. Shields," Lansky says when I walk through the door of senior seminar the next morning. The bell just rang, but he's a total sergeant major about punctuality. "Please find a seat so we can get started."

There's a spot across the room, beside Hannah. Lansky's frown bores into me as I walk past his desk. He's a squat moon-faced man who coaches the school swim team. In fact, he coached Logan. No wonder he doesn't like me.

"Hey," I say when I reach Hannah's side. I allow myself one quick glance at her tight white sweater before I sit down.

"Hey," she says.

Lansky clears his throat. "We'll be pairing off today and continuing with our self-assessment sheets. Your partner will read what you've written and offer their opinion."

Hannah gives me a questioning look. I nod. People start moving chairs, breaking into groups. We slide our desks together.

"The key isn't to criticize," Lansky says. "It's to give constructive feedback. Students are often too harsh in their self-assessments." He starts handing out our work sheets.

"You wanna get together tonight?" Hannah asks.

I stop breathing. Hannah's asking me out?

"I'm taking Amy to a show. You could come."

With *Amy*? My breath starts up again, a gulp of disappointment. I don't want to see Logan's ten-year-old sister. I can't. "I'm working."

"You could meet us for ice cream after."

Hannah's brown eyes look all innocent, but I know what she's doing. She's trying to keep me from going to tonight's race. "I'm busy," I tell her.

She opens her mouth, but I speak first. "I'm not racing. I promised, remember? In the hospital. Never again."

"Then come for ice cream."

Lansky drops our sheets down, taps his finger against mine and gives me a look. "I would like to see more of an effort here, Mr. Shields. Some focus."

"Yeah, yeah," I mutter after he moves on.

"You've written almost nothing," Hannah says when she glances down. "How come?"

At least we aren't talking about the race. "Just lazy, I guess." Her perfume is sending my heart into overdrive. "Let's do yours first."

I skim her strengths (caring and considerate, organized) and her weaknesses (stubborn, opinionated, judgmental). Oh yeah. Especially of me in the last year.

"You're good with sick people too." The doctors were about to amputate my leg in September, but after Hannah visited me in the hospital, I got better.

She blushes. "You think?"

"Yeah. You should write that down." I read her academic strengths and weaknesses before looking at what she's written under *Future Plans*.

I plan to become a kinesiologist because I care about others and I'm interested in the healing professions.

"You should be a doctor," I say when I finish reading.

"That's for Cole, not me."

How perfect that Mr. Perfect is going to graduate and save lives. We're alike in one way at least. I will graduate.

"And anyway, I don't want to be a doctor."

"You should. You go around touching people and they get better." I grin. "Maybe you're a witch."

Her brown eyes turn stormy. "Shut up, Shields."

"Don't worry, I don't think so." She starts to smile. "And judging by the way Cole 'the Mole' Murray looks at you, he doesn't think so either."

Her smile dissolves. "His name is *Cole,* and the way he looks at me is perfectly normal." She snatches up my paper. "We're just friends."

And my day just got a little bit better.

She twirls a curl of hair between her thumb and forefinger as she reads my sheet. I stare at the tiny mole beside her lips, and I grow warm.

Frowning, she looks up. "This is lame."

I pretend to misunderstand. "I know. The whole thing is. I don't need to do this stupid self-assessment."

"I don't mean the sheet. I mean your answers. The only strength you've listed is good with cars." She raises her brow. "What are you going to do? Work for Ray the rest of your life?"

Her comment stings. "We can't all be doctors. Or kinesiologists."

She gestures to the section marked *Future Plans*. "You've left this part blank."

"Give the girl an A."

"Don't be stupid." She leans over to grab my pen. The heat from her body makes my head swim. "What are you doing after graduation?"

Needing air, I inch back. I wish I had something better to say than "I'm going be a licensed mechanic." It sounds like nothing beside Cole "I'm going to be a doctor and save lives" Murray.

She stares at me like I'm a specimen in science class. "This is about Logan, isn't it?"

"No, it's not about *Logan*!" A couple of people turn to stare. I lower my voice. "That's a stupid thing to say."

"It's not. I don't know what's going on in your head."

Good thing. I've been mostly thinking about her breasts in that sweater since I sat down. And telling myself I don't smell cherry Twizzlers. Not at all.

"Maybe you think you don't deserve to go to college or something."

My left eye starts to twitch. "That's lame." And way too close to the truth.

"Okay, fine." She taps the pen against the section marked *Future Plans*. "Well?"

It's now or never. "I'm going to become a licensed mechanic." I stare straight at her, daring her to laugh or wince or roll her eyes.

But all she does is nod her head and start to write. "Good."

I'm shocked. She has accepted, without question, the thing I most want. Even though it probably reminds her of Logan.

"With a good garage," I add. "Maybe even my own some day." Her acceptance has made me nervous. "Just as soon as I can get the money together. Which might take a while, 'cause, you know…I have expenses." Epic understatement.

She finishes writing and looks at me. "You could always sell your car."

You *should* sell it, she's thinking. "It's been in an accident, remember?

I wouldn't get anything for it." Besides, whatever I got, Ray would take.

"Why not apprentice? You could go to school and earn at the same time."

And just like that, Hannah Sinclair gives me the key to my future. And maybe the ticket to getting Ray off my back. "Yeah," I say, "I can be an apprentice."

I wish I could throw my arms around her neck and kiss her lips. I wish I had the hots for someone other than my dead buddy's girlfriend.

The smell of cherry Twizzlers threatens to choke me.

I wish I could make Logan go away.

Chapter Five

I can't wait to talk to Ray about the apprenticeship idea. With any luck, he'll go for it and let me keep my car. Unfortunately, when I get to the garage after school, he's in a lousy mood.

"I'm two cars behind, and everybody wants their job done yesterday." Scowling, he slams the hood on a red Solstice.

"I've barely had time to take a piss, never mind have a smoke." He pulls a cigarette from his overalls and heads for the door. "Make coffee, and if anybody phones, make no promises."

My question will have to wait.

I make the coffee and then get back to work on the 350Z. My phone's in my pocket, set to vibrate. Blair will text me the time and place of the race. The way the cops are, races are never held in the same place twice, so I have no idea where it'll be tonight, other than somewhere in the south end of King County.

Around eight, Ray orders pizza. It's still freaking cold outside, so I convince him to shut the garage door, and we sit by the desk in the corner. I wait until he's eaten three pieces of pepperoni and cracked a beer before I bring up the apprenticeship thing.

"One of my teachers called Mom yesterday." I grab another slice. "About planning for college. Mom wants me to go. She figures I should be an accountant."

His beer can stops midway to his mouth. "Don't tell me you're going to turn into a suit, Shields?" His beady squirrel eyes are glued on me. "*Don't* tell me."

I lick grease from my thumb. "Of course I'm not."

"Whew." The can meets his lips.

"I'm gonna be a licensed mechanic." I wait one heartbeat, two heartbeats. "I was thinking you could take me on as an apprentice. That way I can train while I work."

Ray stares like I've asked him to fly me to the moon. "What?"

I start to repeat myself, but he stops me with an impatient wave of his hand. "I heard. You're already working for me. You're already trained. I don't need you to apprentice. I don't care if you have a license."

I do. I need a license to make decent money. To open my own place some day. "If I line up an apprenticeship, Mom and the teacher will get off my back." Plus, I'll make money while I go to school.

"I don't need the hassle."

"It wouldn't be a hassle." I pop the tab on my can of cream soda and gulp some courage.

"Are you nuts? Sure it would be. I'd have a pile of paper pushers crawling all over this place, looking at how we do things. They might see stuff they don't like." His gaze shifts to a new box of parts that arrived that morning. Hot parts, I'm guessing.

"Plus there'd be all that paperwork to fill out. And they'd probably want to look at my books too." He snorts. "It'll be a cold day in hell before I let anyone see those."

"But I'd be able to work full-time. We could set up a plan to pay back what I owe on the car." And the most important thing—I could keep it.

Ray drains his beer and leans forward, his paunch almost resting on his knees. "It'll be six or eight months before you graduate and enroll in any kind of mechanics program. I ain't waiting that long for my money." He tosses his can toward the rest of the empties in the corner. "Five grand by this time next week, Shields, or ten grand in work. Otherwise your car belongs to me."

That's not happening. And that means I have to convince the guys to get their cars in to Ray.

The text comes just before eleven. *Twenty mins. The old auto wrecking yd. Nr Green Rvr.*

"I gotta go," I tell Ray as I shrug out of my overalls. "I'll be in early tomorrow."

The night is clear. Diamond-bright stars litter the sky as I fly past a string of nurseries, a weathered old barn and berry patches. Soon the fields give way to chain-link fences and industrial parks. A few minutes later my headlights pick out a familiar site looming on my right: ghost cars flattened and stacked like a heap of pancakes. The old wrecking yard.

My heart skips a beat. Is Logan's Lexus in there somewhere? Has it been turned into a ghost car?

I don't want to know.

Rounding the corner, I come face-to-face with a bank of cars parked off the road. The hoods are open, and people are inspecting them. It's a small crowd tonight. Twenty or thirty people. Maybe a dozen cars. I see Luc's Civic.

Blair's Mazda. The red Lancer everybody's talking about. And the white
Porsche Boxster that showed up at Ray's
last night. Interesting. I back in beside
Blair and pop my hood.

"Hey, man, you made it," Blair
says.

"Wouldn't miss it." I stare down
the long straight stretch of pavement.
Tonight's track.

"Come see the Lancer. Driver's name
is Isaac."

Issac is a skinny, pimply-faced guy
with too-long legs and a bad attitude.
"I hear you're the guy to beat," he says
as I lean over to check out his engine.

"Yeah, but I'm not racing. Not
tonight." Not ever.

"Why not? There's three hundred
bucks on the line."

As if I need reminding. Lucas and
Drew wander over, along with a couple

of guys I don't know. Engines are being revved. Tires spin. The air is heavy with the smell of exhaust. "I'm watching. That's all."

"Good thing." He smirks. "You'd lose anyway. I hit a hundred and forty the other night. You'd never beat that."

Blood rushes to my head. He has no idea what I have under my hood. I'm about to say so when I remember why I'm here. To discredit him. To make him nervous. "No way you hit a hundred and forty." I gesture to his hood like his parts are fish guts. "Not with what you have there."

A flush hits his cheeks. Murmuring breaks out behind me. "We clocked him," someone says. "He hit at least a hundred and forty."

"It was a fluke," I say as Santiago, the Boxster driver, joins us. "A one-time thing."

"Yeah?" The flush crawls up Isaac's forehead. "Let's go then. You and me."

Santiago raises his eyebrow. He's enjoying this. I can tell. "I'm not the guy to beat." I point to Santiago. "He is."

Santiago studies me for a second, his dark eyes unreadable. I'm counting on him not being able to resist a challenge. Most of us can't. Finally he turns to Isaac. "I'm in." His thunderbolt tat ripples as he gestures to the track. "What about you?"

Isaac hesitates just a second too long. He's unsettled. Maybe even a little spooked. Which is good. Spooked drivers lose. "For sure," he says.

Hoods are slammed down. Isaac sends a buddy down the track. The two cars pull up to the start line. My pulse starts to hammer. I'm not racing, but I have a lot riding on the outcome.

"Good thing you didn't take your transmission in to his mechanic," I tell Lucas. "From what I saw under that hood, the guy couldn't fix a go-cart."

"You're nuts," Lucas mutters. "The Lancer will take him."

"The Lancer's going to lose." I hope. I stare at the two cars lined up side by side. The Boxster has a rear engine. It'll get better traction off the line. With any luck, Isaac will overcompensate and spin his wheels. I'm counting on it.

Suddenly it's like I'm no longer watching. It's like I'm in the car, ready to race. My blood surges with anticipation, with adrenaline. My foot is poised, as if I'm ready to slam down the gas pedal. Shoot for the finish line.

At the arm drop, the cars fly forward. The Boxster launches smoothly. Isaac struggles for traction and is slow off the start. The Boxster edges ahead.

My heart thrums as I watch the taillights disappear into the darkness. With any luck, the Boxter's lead will hold. A few minutes later, the call comes from the finish line.

"The Boxster took it." Blair's face mirrors shock. "By five car lengths."

"Told you. The other night was beginner's luck." My knees are like butter. "His mechanic sucks." I look at Lucas. "You'd better let Ray do your rebuild."

He nods. "I'll come in tomorrow."

I didn't race. I turned down three hundred in cash. But I've got Lucas coming in for a transmission job. That's five thousand for Ray. I'm halfway to keeping my car.

Chapter Six

Saturday and Sunday my mood goes up and down a dozen times like the elevator at the Space Needle in downtown Seattle.

When I show up for work Saturday morning, Ray's standing beside the coffee machine, waiting for it to finish dripping. Half a dozen homemade muffins sit in a square Tupperware container on the desk. His wife must have baked them.

"I hear you were at the track last night."

His pissed-off tone makes me uneasy. What I do in my spare time is none of his business. "That was fast," I joke. "Did Santiago call you at dawn or what?"

Ray doesn't answer. The coffee machine sputters the last of its brew into the pot. He pours a cup, adds sugar and cream. When he turns, his lips are twisted in disgust. "Why the hell would you hang around the track if you aren't going to race?"

"I can watch, can't I?" I grab a muffin. They're still warm.

Ray scowls. "Why sit and watch when you owe me twenty grand? You should be out there racing."

My anger starts to boil. I put the muffin back down. "I don't need to race. I've got Lucas coming in at ten for a trannie job. That's worth five grand."

He grunts. "Four maybe. Not even half of what I want. And you have less than a week to go." He eyes me over the rim of his mug. "You're gonna lose your car, Tom. It's gonna be mine."

Alarm clutches my gut. "I didn't *ask* you to fix my car. You came to me when I was in the hospital after my second operation. You offered!" Mom didn't like the idea, but when I told her there was no point in having my car in pieces, she agreed. I should've known Ray would attach strings.

"And now I want to be paid."

My rage boils over. "When you fixed it, you said I could take as long as I needed to pay you back. No rush, remember?"

"I've changed my mind."

"That's not fair."

"It's not fair that you changed your mind either."

"What are you talking about?"

"About racing. You used to race. Now you show up and watch."

You kill your best friend and see how you feel about racing afterward. "I didn't change my mind. I stopped. There's a difference. And it's none of your business anyway."

"It is my business. When you race and win with a car I build, my business goes up." He shakes his head. "Plus you pocket three, maybe four grand a month. And you end up with your cut from all the extra business you bring me. It's a no-brainer."

Maybe to him.

"If you raced, you'd have me paid off in six or seven months."

And then I could start helping Mom with my medical bills. I know. I've thought about it. "I'm not racing," I say again. "Lucas will be here at ten. I'll get you another five grand in business by the end of the week."

I take a break when Lucas comes in, mostly to convince Ray to put his other job aside so Lucas can get his car back Sunday. After that, I choke down a muffin, and then I take my phone and shoot a picture of a new engine Ray's dropping into a Honda. Ten minutes after I post it to Facebook, Drew makes a comment and I answer back.

"I'm not paying you to socialize," Ray gripes as the texts start to fly.

But within the hour, I manage to generate enough of a buzz about Ray's work that one of Blair's buddies texts to say he needs a new set of tires and rims and he'll be in the next day at one.

He never shows up. When I text him at two on Sunday, he says he's decided to wait until January. And my mood plunges again. It goes even lower just before five when the white Boxster pulls up to the back door.

"Santiago's here," Ray announces. "I thought we could have some beer."

I don't think so. "I've gotta go." I throw the wrench I'm cleaning into the toolbox. "Mom's got dinner waiting."

Santiago gets out of the car, wanders over to my Acura and spends way too long eyeing it. I pretend not to notice. I slide out of my overalls and hang them up, grab my keys from the desk. "See you Tuesday, Ray."

"Nice set of wheels," Santiago says when I reach the driver's door. He pats my hood and gives me a smile that could freeze fire. The guy's got no warmth whatsoever. Although he must have a wicked high body temp because he's wearing another T-shirt—black this time—and the temperature outside has to be hovering around zero. A challenge dances in his dark brown eyes. "I hear you're the guy to beat."

I glance back at the shop. Ray's watching us. Plotting something. I can tell.

"Not anymore." I slide behind the wheel. "I'm done with racing."

It's true, I vow as I head for home. I'm not racing again. I'll find another way to keep my car.

I drive home on autopilot, not realizing until I see the playground sign up ahead that I've forgotten to take the long way around. I've taken my old route instead, past the elementary school and park, and within a block of Logan's house.

Logan. The prickles start up on my neck. I catch a whiff of cherry Twizzlers. I crank the stereo, hoping bad rock will distract me.

Old Mr. Chang's store is still on the corner. The guy must be 105 by now. I ease up on the gas and check my speed.

The cops used to wait behind Chang's blue dumpster to catch drivers speeding in the school zone. I remember when Chang caught me and Logan stealing bubble gum in grade two. He made us clean out his vegetable bins for an entire week. Logan almost threw up when he touched a bag of rotten carrots.

I can still hear him gag.

At the curb, a woman wearing a puffy red coat raises her arm and signals for me to stop. A badass would boot it through the intersection, but I see a small group of kids waiting behind her so I slow down. Even badasses stop for kids.

Tapping my fingers impatiently on the wheel, I wait for them to cross. They waddle in front of my car like a flock of baby ducks, laughing and shoving and making too much noise. One straggler brings up the rear. She's carrying a grimy basketball and wearing a yellow jacket.

No way. It can't be. Shock waterfalls through me. Amy? What are the odds?

Apparently, pretty good.

I slouch down in my seat, hoping she won't see me.

She's taller, I realize as she passes my car. Her face is sharper too. Maybe because she's older. I haven't seen her since the funeral. But the truth is, that kind of sharpness doesn't come from being older. It comes from sadness.

One of the kids in the group says something to her. She smiles and dips her head toward him. Logan does that. Or he did. Their mom does too.

Tears ball in the back of my throat, and my eyes start to sting. Thank God I'm in the car. Thank God my steel shell is protecting me. I couldn't stand her seeing me like this.

She is past me now, almost to the curb. She still wears her hair in pigtails.

And they are still crooked. Logan always used to razz her about that.

My guts twist. I've taken something from Amy that she'll never get back. Her big brother. No matter how sorry I am, no matter how much good I do for the rest of my life, I can never do enough good to make this right.

Amy steps up on the curb and turns left. The woman in the puffy red jacket waits until all the kids are on the sidewalk before bringing up the rear.

I swallow the lump in my throat and blink back my tears. Then I check my side mirror. And that's when I see it. A flutter of movement. A flash of black hair.

I blink and it's gone.

My hands are shaking. I clutch the steering wheel to keep them still, slowly step on the gas. I'm not imagining things. And I'm not crazy either. It's Logan. He's pissed. He's haunting me.

And I deserve it.

Chapter Seven

I can't eat dinner.

"Roast beef is your favorite," Mom says as she glances at my still-full plate. Becky's almost done. Cam and Becky's boyfriend, Russ, are already on seconds. "What's wrong?"

What's not wrong? "Ray brought in burgers and it was kinda late." True, except I couldn't eat them.

Mom eyes me too closely. "I swear you're losing weight. Maybe you should see the doctor."

What am I going to tell him? That my dead buddy is haunting me? I don't think so.

I force myself to eat a little, though Mom gives me another weird look when I turn down pie. I never turn down pie. Especially not apple.

After I help with the clean up, I park myself in front of the TV with Becky and Russ, suffering through a bunch of reality shows about hoarders and baby beauty contestants and women who didn't know they were pregnant.

There are worse things than not knowing you're pregnant, I decide as I watch them wheel a woman into the operating room. Worse things than losing a car too. Like losing a brother or a son. Like losing a best friend. Seeing Amy reminded me of that.

But it also reminded me that my car is my protection. My safety net. I can't lose it. It's the only thing I have left. The only thing that makes me, me.

Eventually Russ and Cam leave and Mom reminds us that it's a school night, so I have no choice but to head upstairs. I boot up the computer and ignore the prickle that's been tickling the back of my neck since I saw Logan in the crosswalk. Then I do what I always do when I need a distraction: I drive.

Within minutes, I'm screaming through the make-believe streets of Bayview in a red Lamborghini, shooting past hidden hideouts, coming face-to-face with unexpected challengers. I'm totally there, totally present, not thinking of Logan or Amy or my problem with Ray. I'm in control. And the way things are going lately, it's a relief to be in control of something.

Several hours and a couple of successful races later, I'm in the black by thousands of dollars. Too bad real life isn't as simple as *Need for Speed 2*. I shut things down and crawl into bed. Too bad I can't turn Logan off like I turn off the computer.

I can't. And I don't. In fact, I dream of him. We're playing basketball on the school court. He is beating me. We're both laughing. Then he turns serious, deadly. He lunges for my neck and squeezes. I see Drew and Blair and Lucas in the distance. I open my mouth to yell for them but I can't breathe, never mind talk. They don't know…they aren't helping…and then Logan turns into Ray and…

I jerk awake, bolt up in bed, gasp for air. It was a dream, just a dream.

But the smell of cherry Twizzlers almost chokes me.

Heart thudding, I gulp in deep breaths and stare around my bedroom.

I'm searching out familiar shapes in the darkness, praying I don't see *him*. There's my desk, the computer, the mess of clothes I dropped on the floor a few hours ago. They're all where they're supposed to be. *This* is real. *That* wasn't. But it sure felt real. Especially when Logan turned into Ray and when the guys ignored me.

I lie back down and pull the covers almost over my head. They would have come if I'd been able to yell. That's what friends do. They help. I'll talk to them tomorrow. Tell them about Ray. Together we'll come up with a plan. I focus on that thought instead of the smell of cherry Twizzlers wafting through my bedroom.

I get to school early the next morning, but I can't find the guys. I strike out between first and second class too.

After math I see Blair talking to Kate and I'm tempted to interrupt, but then I catch the warning in his eyes and keep on going.

My luck turns at lunch when I find them in the weight room. Blair's doing leg presses, Drew is doing a series of curls and squats with dumbbells and Lucas is goofing around with a ball.

I straddle the weight bench beside Blair. "You know how you want to get your front end lowered?"

He does another leg press and grunts.

I take that as a yes. "I need you to get your car in to Ray this week."

He grunts again and keeps on pressing.

"Can you?"

Blair stops mid-press. The leg press smashes back to home. "Why are you bugging me about this now?" He grabs a towel, wipes a trickle of sweat from his forehead. "I'm trying to work out. Or did you miss that part?"

"Ray's threatening to take away my car," I blurt.

"Holy shit." Lucas stops bouncing.

Drew's dumbbell stops midway to his shoulder. "You're kidding, right?"

"I wish." I jump from the bench, grab a seven-pound hand weight, flip it nervously between my palms. "Ray says if I don't get him five grand in cash or bring in sixty-five hundred dollars' worth of work by Friday, he's taking the Acura."

"He can't do that," Drew says flatly. "That's illegal."

"I owe him twenty grand for the rebuild."

"Are you making payments?"

"Not exactly."

"Then he can," Lucas says.

Luc's mom is a lawyer. I'm betting he's right.

"I can't lose my car."

"Why not?" Blair says. "It's not like you're racing it."

Lucas tries not to laugh and ends up snorting.

"It's my wheels. Cut out my heart, why don't you?" They won't meet my eyes. Not even Drew. Of course, he's probably embarrassed because he doesn't have a car to defend. "How would you like it if someone took your car?"

A weighty silence falls. Luc and Blair look at each other. Drew stares at his feet.

"What can we do?" Blair finally asks.

"You can get your car in this week."

"I can't." Blair holds up his hands when I start to speak. "I'm sorry, okay? Really. But my brother has this big Christmas gift idea for the parents and I told him I'd kick in some cash. I can't do my car until after the holidays."

"There must be guys you know who need work done. Can't you ask around?"

"For sure," Drew says.

"Today," Blair adds.

But ever-practical Lucas says, "It's a long shot. You know that, right?"

"Of course I know that. But I'm desperate. Tell them they'll get a great price. Tell them what a good mechanic Ray is."

Blair gulps from his water bottle. "Even if he is a jerk." He wipes his mouth.

"It's gonna be a hard sell," Lucas says. "Guys are still hot on the new mechanic in Everett. Not so much on Ray these days."

"He did a good job on Luc's trannie," I remind them. "And he did a total rebuild of my Acura."

"Yeah, except..." Luc's voice trails away. *Who knows how it's performing.* I know exactly what he was going to say.

Blair returns his dumbbells to the rack. "You have anything hanging around your house you can sell? My grandmother sold a couple of old paintings and made over three grand."

"Doubt it."

"You should look in your basement," Drew says. "You never know what you'll find. We made twelve hundred bucks in a garage sale last summer."

Luc scowls. "He doesn't have time for a garage sale. It's Monday. Ray wants the cash by Friday."

"Who said anything about a garage sale, dweeb?" Drew turns to me. "Hey, it was just an idea. Secondhand stores buy stuff all the time."

"It's a good idea. Anything helps." I return the hand weights to the rack, mentally review the contents of my basement. I'm sure there's a box of old ski equipment down there. Piles of books. "I'll have a look."

Blair unfolds himself from the weight machine. "We'll get on it right away," he says as he heads for the door. "There's no way we can let a prick like Ray take your car from you."

"No way," Drew and Lucas echo.

As I follow them into the hall, I'm almost grateful for my nightmare. And I'm certainly grateful for my friends.

Chapter Eight

That afternoon, Hannah hits me with a bomb. And she does it in senior seminar.

"I saw Amy on Friday," she whispers.

And I saw her yesterday. Nausea turns my stomach inside out. But I don't want to talk about her. I'd rather talk about the assignment Lansky has given us.

Ten minutes to write two paragraphs on who we'd like to have as a mentor in our second semester. "I know. You took her to a show."

"Yeah."

I frown at my paper, pretending to be thinking hard. I've written Ray's name down, with a big question mark. Hannah, I note out of the corner of my eye, has finished her two paragraphs.

"She's doing okay," she adds.

How okay can she be? She's lost her big brother forever.

Hannah fiddles with her pencil. "She asked about you."

Sweat beads on my forehead. "Right." I don't want to know. I cross out Ray's name and write down Cam instead. He's a bus driver. Probably not the kind of mentor Lansky has in mind, but Cam's honest and he's smart.

"She wants me to ask you to come to Logan's party."

My head jerks up. "Logan's party?" Lansky is staring in our direction. I lower my voice. "What party?"

"Logan would have turned eighteen in December." She taps her pencil lightly against her desk. "Amy wants to hold a party for him."

Another roll of nausea. This one makes me full-on queasy. Maybe I'm coming down with the flu. Or maybe I'm sick with guilt. "You're kidding, right?"

"No." Hannah shakes her head. "She's having a party. Her parents have said it's okay. Amy wants you to come. They all do."

My heart skips a beat. Like I believe that. Not. "Logan's dead. A party's a dumb idea."

"Maybe, but they're having one and Amy wants you there."

She might want me there, but for sure her parents don't.

"What should I tell her?"

"Tell her no."

"You won't go?"

"I won't go."

Hannah puts her pencil down. "Why not?"

"I just can't."

A veil of disappointment falls over her face. "Please?"

"No." It was bad enough seeing her on the street when I was inside my steel safety net. I can't walk into Logan's house and see her there. See his parents. I can't take another reminder of what I did.

"I'll be there too," she adds.

And that's supposed to help? Logan was Hannah's boyfriend. I don't need a reminder of that either. I shake my head.

She turns away, but not before I glimpse the flicker of disgust in her eyes.

Lansky stops me after class. First I think it's because Hannah and I were talking too much. Then I think it's because he's seen that my assignment is incomplete. As I brace myself for another lecture, he says, "I went over the self-assessment sheets you finished Friday. I see you've picked a direction. You want to be a licensed mechanic."

Now it's coming, I think. The lecture. The reminder that I could do better.

"So I dug up some information for you."

Huh?

He holds out some brochures. Lansky's helping me? He's barely been civil since Logan died.

He flaps the papers. "Inside you'll find some of the technical colleges that offer the courses you'll need to become a licensed mechanic. It appears the two best contenders are Renton Tech or Bellingham Tech."

Realizing this isn't some kind of joke, I take the material. His fingers are squat, like him, but his nails are perfect rectangles, and shiny. Lansky gets manicures? It's just one surprise on top of another.

"Don't look so shocked, Mr. Shields." He says my name like he's calling me *Mr. Turd*. "It's my job. I'm paid to find this stuff out."

I guess civility is too much to expect. "Thanks."

He reaches for his briefcase, gathers up his papers.

"I, uh, I'm thinking of becoming an apprentice." I'm not sure why I'm telling him this. Maybe he'll know someone? Maybe I want him on my side when I tell Mom? Maybe both.

"Look at Renton then. They have an apprenticeship program." He grabs his brown blazer from the back of his chair.

"There are lots of opportunities out there for you." His bulbous blue eyes fasten on my face. "As long as you don't screw up." *Again*, he is thinking. I can read his mind. "And are willing to work hard."

His squat little body disappears out the door.

Hard work is the least of my worries. It's holding on to my car that's the problem. A puff of breath hits the back of my neck. I shiver. And figuring out how to get rid of a ghost.

After school, I crank my iPod and head down to the basement to see what I can find to sell. I spend the first five minutes sneezing and looking nervously over my shoulder, expecting Logan to jump out of the corner. He doesn't. No surprise. The guy never liked dark places. Or hard work.

And since our basement is the size of a small apartment, going through it is hard work.

After a couple of hours, I find a box of used tools Ray unloaded on me last year, a couple of pairs of skis that are too small and an ancient guitar that belonged to my mom when she was a kid. Acoustic, not electric, but when I brush the dust off I see nice wood and pearl inlay. In the old bathroom, I find a carton of dusty books. Under a pile of blankets by the back door, I discover an old oak rocker with cool carved arms that apparently belonged to my grandmother. Mom doesn't want the stuff. She says I can go ahead and sell it.

Tuesday and Wednesday, I make the rounds of secondhand stores. I manage to pull together almost three hundred bucks. I spend my nights playing more *Need for Speed 2*, my days hustling work.

I find someone who needs a new exhaust system, and the guys find someone who needs a cold-air intake system. It's good but not good enough. The two jobs together don't even total a grand.

Thursday, with my panic edging into the red zone, Blair and the others help me brainstorm how I can convince Ray to give me more time. Blair also offers to write Ray a note.

"What are you going to do?" I ask as we eat our lunch in the cafeteria. "Beg for me?"

"You wish." Blair stuffs a third of a burger into his mouth. It's a full minute before he can talk. "I'll promise to bring my car in after the holidays."

"That's not enough."

"It's the best I can do."

I hand him a paper and a pen.

"You still have twenty-four hours," Lucas reminds me. He points to my fries. "You gonna eat those?"

Wordlessly I slide them across the table. I still can't eat.

"That's right," Drew says. "Maybe somebody will turn up tomorrow needing a new engine."

"Maybe, but I doubt it." And I can't wait until tomorrow. I need to talk to Ray today.

Chapter Nine

I almost chicken out.

What's the big deal about waiting another day? I wonder after I get to the garage and see what job Ray has lined up for the afternoon. Maybe something will happen in twenty-four hours.

Like a miracle.

But I can't live like this. I have to settle the car thing. Then I can put my energy into getting Logan off my back.

I approach Ray when he stops for a coffee and a smoke. "Here." I dig Blair's note out of the pocket of my overalls and slap it, along with the three hundred dollars, on the desk in front of him.

Ray peers through a veil of cigarette smoke. "What the hell's that?"

I straddle the chair beside the desk and work at keeping my voice casual. "Three hundred bucks I raised by selling every single piece of useless shit I could find in my basement."

He laughs. "Don't tell me. You want me to put that toward your debt?"

"Yes." I point to the paper. "And that's from Blair promising to bring in his Mazda by the end of January so you can lower his front end."

"What good's that gonna do me?"

"Lots in January when business is slow. The kind of front-end work Blair wants will bill out at two grand, easy."

"So?"

A gust of wind rattles the metal pull-down door. I almost jump. "So in the last week I've brought in almost six grand worth of work, three hundred bucks in cash, and the promise of two grand more in another month or so."

Ray slurps from his yellow Happy Face mug. "That's not the ten grand I wanted."

"It's close."

"Close isn't good enough."

I will myself not to panic. "Taking my car away is going to mess you up, big time."

He puffs on his cigarette. "What do you mean?"

"I know a lot of people. Everybody will know what you've done."

He's silent.

"You think business is down now? Watch what happens when word gets out that you took my car. That you left me with no wheels. You aren't going to be popular."

"Who said anything about leaving you with no wheels?"

"Don't mess with me, Ray." He's twisting things, like he always does. "You've made it pretty clear that if I don't come up with what you want by tomorrow, my car belongs to you."

"That's right. It will. But you won't be without wheels. You can drive the shop car whenever you want."

Great. A rusty old Ford.

"And it's not like you'll never see your Acura again," he adds. "It'll be around. It'll still be a contender."

I'm trying to remember what else the guys told me to say, so at first his words don't register. But when they do, a shiver creeps up my spine. "What do you mean, my car will be around?"

"I'm not getting rid of it. That thing's a moneymaker. I'll find someone else to race it a couple nights a week."

Someone else will race *my* car? I grit my teeth. No way.

Ray smirks. "One of your friends, maybe?"

My stomach clenches. "I don't think so."

"'Course, there is an alternative."

"What's that?"

He guzzles the last of his coffee, plops the mug on the desk. "You quit being an ass and race it yourself."

"Forget it."

"I'll pretend I didn't hear that." He squishes his cigarette butt under the toe of his boot, leans forward and pins me with a look. "I'm setting up an organized illegal for Sunday night. Out at the old

Macmillan airstrip. Santiago's racing. Against your car."

I stare at Ray. My Acura will take the Boxter, easy. And Ray knows it.

"Your car is going in that race. Either you drive it or someone else will." He pauses for a heartbeat. "I'd rather it was you."

"Why me?"

"'Cause you're good. 'Cause you owe me." He smiles. "And 'cause you ain't the guy who died."

It's the kind of reminder I don't need.

"Santiago's throwing in three grand, and I'm matching him. Winner takes it."

My heart skips a beat. "Six grand? On a *single* race?"

Ray nods. "That's right. 'Course, your car will belong to me by then, so I'll get the whole shebang."

So this is the con. Ray's setting Santiago up. He knows the Boxter's no match for my Acura.

"You win and I'll wipe a thousand dollars off your debt." Ray winks. "I'll even give you a few more months to pay me off. How's that for a deal?"

It's a sweet deal. It's only one race. Just one. And for sure I'd win.

The door rattles. This time I do jump.

But I've promised Hannah. Promised myself. "No."

Ray waves my answer away. "You've got till tomorrow to decide. Sleep on it."

I don't need to sleep on it. I'm not racing again. No way.

But that means Ray takes my car.

When I get home later that night, I'm scared and I'm angry. I'm out of options. I'm losing my car, and I have no one to blame but myself.

I hear the murmur of Mom's voice as I open the door and hang my jacket on the coatrack. Then Cam says, "It'll work out. Something will come up."

I stop midway through slipping off my shoes. It's like he's talking right to me.

"No." Mom's voice sounds thready and too high, like she's been crying. "It's the right thing to do. I've decided."

I walk down the hall to the kitchen. They're sitting at the table, bent over mugs of coffee and a pad of paper. "Decided what?"

Mom's head jerks up. "Oh, Tom. Hi." Her green eyes are overly bright as she glances at the wall clock. "Wow. Is it that time already?"

"Decided what?" I open the fridge, scan the contents.

"Nothing's been decided." Cam has a deep, gravelly voice that matches his six-foot-three build and dark brown beard. "Your Mom's thinking through some options, that's all."

"What options?" At least she *has* options.

Cam doesn't answer. Instead, Mom says, "There's leftover lasagna if you want it."

"Maybe later." I grab the milk, root through the cupboard for a glass.

"Hannah came by and left an envelope for you," Mom says. "I left it on the hall table."

"Hannah was here?"

"Yes. She was with Amy."

A splash of milk hits the counter.

"Something about a party for Logan," Mom adds. "They want you to go. The details are there."

I shove the carton back in the fridge, grab the dishrag and wipe up the spill. "Thanks. I'll take a look." I head for the door.

"Tom?" Cam's voice causes me to turn around.

He looks fierce, but he's not. He's never judged me. Not once. "Yeah?"

"It may be hard for you to believe, but trust me, you usually regret the things you don't do more than the things you do." He gives me a half smile. "And sometimes we're asked to do hard things to help others. Not that I'm telling you what to do, get it?"

But in other words, go to the party. "Yeah."

I head back down the hall, pick up the envelope on the table and slide my finger under the flap. *A celebration of Logan Freemont's life*, I read. *December 16. Gifts not needed.*

Out in the kitchen, Mom's voice is edging up again. I linger a minute, shuffling through the pile of bills. There's one from the hospital with a big red word stamped across the top: *Overdue.*

Shame worms through me. That bill is my fault.

"I have to, Cam. Seriously. With my hours cut, I just can't do it."

Mom's hours have been cut?

"There's no way I can handle things now."

Handle my bills, she means. A flush hits my cheeks. Here I am worrying about losing my car when Mom is worrying about paying my medical bills. I'm as bad as Ray. Thinking only of myself.

"You can't talk me out of it," Mom adds.

Talk her out of what?

Cam answers. I strain to hear but can't. An official-looking letter from the bank catches my eye. When I skim its contents, my blood stops.

I read the letter twice to make sure I understand. But there's no mistaking it. Mom's borrowed against the house.

"You saw that letter from the bank," Mom says when Cam finishes. "I'm way behind on the mortgage. If I don't come up with five thousand dollars by the end of December, I could lose this place. Selling is my only choice."

Sweat beads on my forehead. Mom's selling the house? Because of me? No way. I can't let that happen. I won't.

Chapter Ten

I have to go back to racing.

The thought needles me as I go upstairs, log on to the computer, surf Facebook and check my email. I can make money racing. Lots of it. Except, I made a promise. And racing is wrong.

Or is it? Stealing is wrong. I'm not sure racing is. Not if it's done right. Not if there's a good reason for it.

After a while, Cam's footsteps echo down the sidewalk outside. His truck pulls out of the driveway. Mom comes upstairs and turns on the shower.

You usually regret the things you don't do more than the things you do.

I'll regret it for the rest of my life if I don't help Mom. And I'm sick of having regrets.

I have to go back to racing.

As the idea grows, my appetite roars to life. I head downstairs to nuke the lasagna. While it heats, I grab the pad of paper Mom left on the table and I begin to write.

No racing with passengers.

No racing while drunk, stoned or tired.

No racing someone who doesn't want to race me.

The microwave *pings*. I pull out my pasta, fork up mounds of noodles and meat and cheese, and study my list.

After a minute, I add: *No racing someone who has passengers, or is drunk, stoned or tired.*

By the time I've finished my second helping of lasagna, I have my rules and my game plan figured out. I need to talk to Ray. He needs to agree to what I want.

Yawning, I head upstairs to bed. I'm full, I'm tired and I'm relaxed. For once, I have a plan. For once, Logan isn't anywhere around. And for once I don't turn on the computer. Instead I go straight to bed.

Straight to sleep.

I'm waiting at the garage when Ray drives up before eight the next morning.

"What the hell?" His checkered shirt catches on the steering wheel as he twists out of his classic Mustang. In street clothes, he's almost skinny. Except for his beer gut. "You off school today?"

"No, my first class is in twenty minutes. But I need to talk to you."

He fumbles with his keys before finding the right one and unlocking the pull-down door. "I don't talk to anybody before I've had my first cup of coffee." The door clatters when it hits the top of the frame.

"I'm short on time and you need to hear this."

Ray flips on the light and bolts for the coffee machine, weaving between a way-cool Nissan Skyline and a yellow Miata. "Oh yeah?"

"I'm going back to racing."

He turns around. A grin splits his face. "I knew you couldn't resist."

"On a couple of conditions."

"What kind of conditions?"

"If I win Sunday, I get the six grand, I keep my car and you wipe out my debt." He stares at me, his grin slowly fading. I pull a sheet of paper from my pocket.

"Plus you sign this saying the Acura is mine, free and clear."

He scowls. "Are you on drugs or what? I'm not signing nothing." He takes the coffee pot to the sink, fills it with water. "I told you yesterday, you go back to racing, I'll give you a few more months to pay me back. And I'll forgive a thousand dollars of your debt. That's enough."

It's not. This isn't about me or my car. Not anymore. It's about Mom. Our house. About fixing the mess I created. I need more. And I'm determined to get it.

"Forget it then." I shrug, like I don't care. "But just so you know, I've told everybody how you're putting the screws to me. Nobody's going to race my car, Ray. You won't get your business back. Not without me behind the wheel." I head for the door.

"Hold on to your bloody shirt, will ya?"

I settle on a stool and watch him make coffee.

When he's finished, he asks, "What's your bottom line?"

If I tell him, he'll weasel me lower. "I need money fast," I say instead. Something close to sympathy flickers in his black squirrel eyes. "And I need you to wipe out my debt."

He pulls a cigarette from his pocket. "Wipe out fourteen grand?" He snorts. "I don't think so."

I pretend to think. "Then give me two years to pay you back. And put it in writing." I'm not settling for a verbal agreement.

"A year," he counters as he lights up and takes a drag.

"Twelve months, but I still want it in writing."

"I don't do signatures."

"It's a deal breaker, Ray. I need something signed."

"Fine," he mutters after a minute. "Whatever."

"And I want that six grand when I win."

"No way."

"Okay." My heart's pounding as I stand up. "Deal's off."

"Don't be an ass, Shields."

I'm no hero. I know that. I can't wipe out my entire medical bill. I can't save the house if Mom decides to sell it. But I want to hand Mom five grand by the end of December. And I want a nice chunk of change from Sunday's race.

"I'll give you a grand," Ray says.

It's tempting, but not enough. "Nope." I start to walk.

"Two then," Ray snarls.

Two grand. Oh man...my heart's thudding so hard that if I looked down, I'm pretty sure I'd see my chest moving. I keep walking.

"Give it to me, Shields," Ray yells. "Your bottom line."

I stop. "Five grand."

"You *are* on drugs. I'm putting up three grand. Why should I walk away with a thousand bucks?"

I turn around. "Think of it as an investment."

His face is stained an angry red. "An investment?"

"In our racing partnership."

Ray stares at me so long I'm afraid I've blown it. Finally he says, "Three and three. I break even. You're ahead. You get your damned signed piece of paper. And you keep racing. That's my final offer, Shields. Take it or leave it."

I pretend to consider. "Okay. But I don't start paying you back the fourteen grand until February."

"For Christ's sake, when did you turn into such a hard-ass?"

"When I started working for you."

A look of grudging respect flares in his eyes. "You got yourself a deal."

Hard-ass. Badass. He can call me what he wants. I'll have three grand on Sunday. Getting another two grand by the end of December will be a cake walk.

Friday's rotation means Hannah and I don't have any classes together. Good, because I don't know what I'll say to her about the racing thing. If I'm lucky, maybe she'll never find out.

I can dream, right?

I avoid her all morning. At lunch, I'm dumping my books in my locker and planning to escape to DQ for a burger when I hear her voice behind me.

"There you are."

I slam my locker shut, twirl my combination. "Hey." She's standing way too close, her thin fingers clutching her books.

I stare at them instead of her face. Heat creeps into my cheeks when I think about how they touched me in the hospital. I glance up at her lips. The flush spreads to my ears.

"You okay?"

"Yeah, fine." People stream down the hall behind us, laughing and talking, relieved that the weekend is almost here. I smell pepperoni. Someone has unwrapped a sandwich.

"I'm glad I caught you."

She's glad she caught me. Maybe she'll ask me out again. Without Amy this time. Maybe we can go to a movie or for a walk and I can explain why I'm going to race again...

"I dropped an invitation off at your place the other night. For Logan's party." She's not looking at me. She's looking over her shoulder and down the hall.

"I got it. Thanks."

"Okay. Good." Her head snaps back to mine. "That's all I wanted to know. Will you at least think about it?"

I don't need to think about it. I'm not going to a party for a guy I killed. But guilt about going back to racing makes me say, "Sure."

Delight sweeps her face. "That's great!" She lurches forward, and for a second I imagine she's going to kiss me, but instead she grabs my arm and squeezes. "I hope you come."

Will you feel that way when you find out I'm racing again, I wonder.

"Oh, there's Cole." She flashes me a second smile. "I'll talk to you later, 'kay?"

As she flies down the hall toward him, the sweet smell of cherry Twizzlers hits my nose. A familiar prickle crawls up the back of my neck. I glimpse ink-black hair.

My breath stops. Logan.

Time...people...everything moves in slow motion.

He's there and then he's gone. I gulp in fast, shallow breaths as I search the crowd for him. Nothing. My breath starts to slow. I was imagining things.

Hannah reaches Cole's side. He pulls her into the crook of his arm and kisses her temple. My heart lurches. *No way.* They're just friends.

Movement flickers off to my left. The Twizzlers smell is almost overpowering. Another prickle hits my neck. I whirl around just in time to see Logan's frown, to see that familiar dip of his head toward Hannah and Cole.

I blink. And he's gone.

But in that second, everything falls into place like a piston sliding into its cylinder. Logan isn't pissed that I killed him. He's pissed that I have the hots for Hannah. He's telling me to leave her alone. He's telling me that she belongs with Cole.

Chapter Eleven

I should be happy. Everything's working out.

I'm keeping my car. I'll have five grand by the end of December, easy. Except, Hannah and Cole? What's good about that?

Nothing.

I keep a low profile for the next couple of days. I don't play pool with the guys Friday night. I don't answer their text about the status of my car. I even skip Luc's party Saturday. I drive to the airstrip instead.

I need to get used to the track. I drive the runways for a couple of hours, memorizing bumps and surface flaws and thinking through possible moves. By the time I'm finished, I have every angle covered.

Sunday dawns cold and wet. It pours all morning. By lunch the rain eases to drizzle, but the temperature drops. When I look out the window at one point, snow is mixed with the rain. Nerves clutch my stomach. The race can't be canceled.

Just before dinner, the weather breaks. An hour later, I get word that the race is on. I'm golden. I'm pumped. I have a race to win!

The temperature is near freezing when I head out around eight. I can't see stars. I know the sky is still overcast.

As long as the rain holds off for another few hours. That's all I care about.

Adrenaline surges when I drive through the broken gate at the old airstrip. Several hundred people have shown up. My mouth is suddenly dry. There have to be fifty or sixty cars here.

I pull up left of the orange cones that mark the starting line. Lucas slaps me on the back when I join them. "Welcome back, Shields. Ray told us you'd be here."

My heart starts to hammer. "He did?" Does Hannah know? *It doesn't matter*, my badass self taunts. *She's with Cole, remember?*

I pop the hood on my car and spend the next fifteen minutes answering questions about my modifications. When Ray comes by, I give him full credit. A few minutes before race time, I'm about to slide behind the wheel when a familiar voice calls my name.

"Tom!"

I look over my shoulder. My knees turn to putty. Hannah is heading straight for me. Her hair's a mess, and the collar on her jean jacket is sticking up at a weird angle. Like she dressed in a hurry.

"I came to see if it was true," she says when she reaches my side. I glance past her for Cole, but he's not there. "To see if you're really racing again."

My tongue won't work. What am I supposed to say? Yes, I'm racing, but it's none of your business. You're with Cole. Or you should be. "I didn't want you to find out this way."

"Oh, really?" She angles her hands on her hips. "How did you want me to find out?"

I didn't. But I can't tell her that.

She stares at me like I'm a piece of toxic waste. "I cannot believe it."

"Look, it's—" I stop. *Necessary*. But I don't have time to explain. "There's a reason I'm here. A bunch of stuff is going on. You don't know the whole story."

"Story?" She takes a sharp, ragged breath and shuts her eyes. When she opens them, they shine like dark chocolate. "The only story I know is that Logan is dead because you challenged him to a race."

I can't afford to think about Logan. I can't get rattled right now.

"And now you're doing it again," Hannah adds.

As if on cue, Santiago pulls his white Boxster up to the starting line. "This is different." I incline my head. "He wants to be here. That's one of my rules. No racing someone who doesn't—"

She cuts me off. "I don't want to know."

Santiago gets out of his car, gives us a curious look. I turn my back to him. "I need money. For my—"

She stops me a second time. "It's just an excuse."

"It's not." My hands are shaking. I feel like I'm going to puke. It shouldn't matter what Hannah thinks. But it does.

She rolls her eyes. "It is. You'll never change. You'll never stop."

"Yes, I will! I'm—"

"Then stop," she says. "Right now. Don't race."

I can't. I just stare at her.

Her lip curls. "I knew it." She stalks off.

Santiago wanders over. He's wearing a leather jacket and a huge ring on his pinky finger. "Nice ass," he says, gazing after her.

His comment slams me like a fist to the gut. "She's taken." I can't think about Hannah right now. I have a race to win.

I get in my car and pull up beside the Boxster. There's a pair of cars ahead of us. We're second.

Santiago smirks and gives me a little salute as he gets behind the wheel. The guy's an idiot. He has money and attitude but no racing smarts. I look over at his competition tires. They're dangerous. A stupid choice for this kind of weather. Ray's a jerk for conning him out of three grand. Making him think he can win. I feel a stab of guilt for going along with it.

A driver I recognize from Burien comes to the start line. He gives the cars in front the signal. My heart kicks into overdrive as I watch the two drivers get ready to launch. Beside me, Santiago is checking his gauges, fiddling with his wheel. He'd better be careful. If he hits a patch of ice, he could lose control, big time.

The two cars shoot off. After a minute, Santiago and I pull ahead. This is it.

I clutch the steering wheel, feather my foot over the gas pedal. And I watch.

The starter raises his arm. And then he drops it.

I launch in a surge of adrenaline and speed. The world rushes by. Blood roars in my ears. Santiago is inches back. I'm going to win. I deserve to win.

And that's when I smell it—cherry Twizzlers. The familiar prickle hits the back of my neck. There's a flash of movement off to my right. It's Logan. Staring at me from the passenger seat. One side of his face is cut and bleeding, the other is smashed beyond recognition.

"Hey, Shields." He grins. "How's it goin'?"

I stop breathing. "You're not real," I yell. "You can't be."

But the look he gives me is as real as anything I've ever seen. I'm pretty sure the blood on his face is wet too.

"Don't be such a dweeb. I'm as real as you are. Probably more."

I swear I'm going to piss my pants. "Go away!"

"No way." He laughs. "I've been trying to get your attention for weeks."

He has it now. Outside the car, everything slows. I'm inching down the track. The world creeps past in major slow motion. Rain is starting to fall; it hovers above the windshield, almost suspended in time.

"Why won't you leave me alone?" A bead of sweat rolls down my forehead and stings my eye. I press on the gas, urge the Acura forward. The car shudders but stays almost still. I can't lose. I need to help Mom. I need my pride. "You're dead."

"And you think life stops when you're dead?" He laughs. "That's naïve."

"I killed you." Tears clog the back of my throat. "If it wasn't for me, you'd still be alive."

He snorts. "You didn't kill me. If you hadn't dared me to race, I would've found another way to bail on life. The same way you are."

"I'm not bailing."

"Sure you are. You're a loser, Shields. A total and complete wuss."

I grit my teeth. "I'm no wuss. Wusses don't race."

"No. They're afraid to live. Just like you. You're scared you don't measure up."

"You're full of it."

"You think you're nothing without five thousand pounds of steel between you and the world."

The tears start to fall.

"You're racing out of fear. All of your decisions are based on fear. Every single one."

"No way." Furiously I wipe my eyes.

"Yes way. You're scared you'll lose your car. You're scared you'll lose your house. You're scared you'll lose Hannah."

"I can't lose Hannah. Hannah doesn't want me. And she's with Cole anyway."

"Yeah, and why do you think I've been bugging you?" He doesn't wait for me to answer. "Cole Murray is a dipstick. You're the one who's supposed to be with Hannah."

"Me?"

He glances over his shoulder. "I don't see anybody else in the car."

You'll never change. You'll never stop.

"Hannah wants me to stop racing. Forever."

He nods. "Yeah."

I'd have to give up my car. I wouldn't be able to help Mom. My stomach bottoms out. What if I give it all up, and Hannah still doesn't want me? Logan's right. I am afraid. I'm afraid I'll never been good enough for Hannah Sinclair.

"I can't do it," I admit.

Logan dips head the way he used to. For a second I forget about his blood and ripped skin and exposed flesh. I see Logan, my friend. And I miss him.

"Wuss," he says again.

Wuss, badass—what's the difference?

Time is speeding up. I catch fifth gear and floor it. There's a surface dip ahead that'll be full of rain. I'll need to compensate. I glance in my rearview mirror.

Santiago won't be able to. Not with those tires. He'll fishtail. Maybe lose control. Panic clutches me. And this crash will be my fault. Because I can see it coming.

I need to stop. It's the only way to get him to slow down. To keep him safe. But if I do…My panic swells, black and heavy. If I do, I'll lose my car, my chance to help Mom, my pride. I'll lose everything.

"He's gaining on you," Logan says.

I glance in the rearview mirror again. But I might save a life.

"What're you gonna be, Shields? A winner or a loser?"

I hit the brakes. Logan smiles and starts to fade.

Chapter Twelve

By the time I pull over, Logan's gone. Santiago slows as he passes me, then disappears down the track. After I stop shaking, I put the car in gear and drive to the finish line, coasting to a stop within inches of Ray.

He yanks open my door. "What the *hell*?" His face is so red it looks like he's sweating blood. "Santiago says you pulled over. Have you lost your mind?"

Have I? I clutch my keys, get out of the car, stare at the passenger seat. What am I looking for? Some kind of sign that what I saw was real? That I'm not a nut job? The seat's empty. There's no sign of life. Or death.

"I just lost three grand!" Ray says.

I know. I lost three grand too. A strange kind of calm settles on me. But I couldn't have lived with myself feeling responsible for another crash.

Over by the Boxster, Santiago looks both smug and pissed. No wonder. It's one thing to win a race. It's another to have a race win handed over.

Except, I didn't just hand him the race. I handed him his life.

"What were you thinking?" Ray demands.

That I'm no loser, no wuss. That I'm through with being a badass. But Ray wouldn't understand. "Nothing." My breath comes out in a puff of white. My keys stab my hand. I hardly understand myself. I wonder if Hannah will.

Engines rumble in the distance. Another race is about to start. There'll always be another race. But not for me. I stare at my Acura. From now on, I'll be without wheels. It'll be just…me. I dangle my keys. "Here." I drop them into Ray's palm. "It's yours."

Giving up my car a few weeks ago was the hardest thing I've ever done. Until now.

Standing on the sidewalk in front of Logan's house, I stare at his front porch. Someone has tied blue balloons to the railing. Cars crowd the driveway and stretch down the street. I had to park Cam's truck two blocks away.

Snow crunches under my feet as I walk up to the front door. Through the window to my right, I see a crowd of people in the living room. A silver Happy Birthday banner hangs from the fireplace. Beads of sweat pop out on my forehead. It would take me two minutes to walk back to the truck, to drive away.

I don't have to be here.

Wuss.

I hear the word like someone is standing beside me. Is it Logan? I'm not sure. I don't feel a prickle. I don't smell Twizzlers. But he's around. I feel him. Especially when I see Hannah.

She and I haven't said more than a dozen words to each other since the race. She's either with Cole or she's ignoring me. Not cool. Fingers shaking, I ring the bell.

Amy answers, staring up at me with those familiar gray eyes. She looks so much like Logan. Tears jam the back of my throat. I want to turn around and run.

But there's nowhere to hide. Nothing to hide behind.

"Tom!" She throws herself at me. "I haven't seen you in, like, forever."

I saw Amy the other day, but she hasn't seen me since the funeral. I clutch her tiny shoulders, swallow back my tears. Amy doesn't hate me. And all this time I thought she did.

"Come on." She tugs me forward. "Mom's back here somewhere. So's the food." My eyes scan the living room as we head for the kitchen. The brown couch is in the same place. The piano's still in the corner. There's the picture of Logan and his family on top. Logan's grandpa is talking to a few of Logan's friends from the swim team. I avoid their eyes. I need to find Hannah and say what I came to say. Before Logan jumps out and spooks me all over again.

"There's the food." Amy points to the table. It's loaded with Swedish meatballs, pasta salad, cheese and crackers. And Hannah is standing beside it.

She's setting out a plate, removing plastic wrap. She's wearing a dress. A tight red dress. Red was Logan's favorite color.

I walk up behind her, thinking of all the things I want to say. *I'll never race again. I promise. Cole's a dipstick. Logan said so.* And: *I saw him and he's still alive and he's okay with us being together.*

Yeah, that'll so fly.

Instead I say, "You can't ignore me forever."

She whirls around. "You came."

"I told you I would. I left three messages. And I texted. Four times."

Her cheeks flood with color. She straightens a tray of veggies and dip. "I've been busy."

Yeah. With Cole "the Dipstick" Murray.

"Here." She hands me a paper plate. "There's cake."

It has blue frosting and it's shaped like a swimming pool. An edge of brown peeks out. Chocolate. Prickles hit my neck. Logan's favorite. The air shifts. My stomach flips. Oh man…I need to get out of here. "You want to get together after school this week?" I ask. "Tuesday or Wednesday? We could go somewhere for fries. And talk."

"There's nothing to talk about."

I won't take no for an answer. "DQ maybe? 'Cause we'll need to walk."

"Yeah, I heard your car is in Ray's shop." She leans over and cuts a piece of cake. Her hair is getting longer. It's past her ears. Soon it'll be touching her shoulders. "Getting fixed or something."

That's what I've told everybody else. Other than Mom and Cam. I wanted Hannah to be the first to know the truth. "Ray owns my car now. It's his."

"Right." Hannah's brown eyes are filled with disbelief as she grabs a fork and straightens. "You gave it away."

"Yeah." The air shifts again. I feel lightheaded. Focus, focus. "I owed him fourteen grand for the repairs, which is one reason I—" I stop. Hannah doesn't need to hear my excuses. There was the car and there was the house. Which we may end up keeping after all if Mom puts a suite in the basement and gets approved for some home-owner-help thing the government has in place.

"I signed it over to him," I tell her. "It's his."

Our gazes lock. She still doesn't believe me. I can tell. "I'm not working for him anymore either."

She blinks. "You're not?"

I shake my head. "I finished two days ago. I start at that garage by the ravine in another week." Ray's biggest competition. Unbelievably, Lansky wrote me a letter of recommendation, and there might even be a chance of an apprenticeship. "Lots has changed, Hannah. I've ch—"

A familiar smell floods the kitchen. Cherry Twizzlers. My heart kicks into overdrive; prickles race down my spine. I brace myself for the flash of black hair, his grin. Instead Amy bounces up to the table, waving a handful of familiar red sticks.

"We forgot the cherry Twizzlers! And we can't have a party for Logan without them." She piles the licorice beside the cake and rushes off again.

My heartbeat slows, but prickles still tease the back of my neck. "So, what's it going to be? Tuesday or Wednesday?"

I'm not giving her a chance to say no. We'll be together sooner or later. It may as well be sooner.

Hannah doesn't answer; she just stares at me. My cheeks grow warm.

I pick up a Twizzler and spin it between my fingers. "We'll go to DQ," I say. "I'll buy you a Snickers Blizzard." The prickles start to fade. "That's your favorite, right?"

"How did you know?"

I smile. "I just did." And the prickles are gone.

"Let's go Wednesday," she says. "I'll drive."

Acknowledgments

With thanks to Bryan Harrison of Evo Street Racers and to Barry Nazarko for the hours of input.

Laura Langston is the author of *Exit Point* and *Hannah's Touch* in the Orca Soundings series, as well as picturebooks and teen novels. Laura lives in Victoria, British Columbia.